MMF

David L. Kimple

A SAMUEL FRENCH ACTING EDITION

SAMUEL FRENCH

FOUNDED 1830

SAMUELFRENCH.COM
SAMUELFRENCH-LONDON.CO.UK

MUSIC USE NOTE

Licensees are solely responsible for obtaining formal written permission from copyright owners to use copyrighted music in the performance of this play and are strongly cautioned to do so. If no such permission is obtained by the licensee, then the licensee must use only original music that the licensee owns and controls. Licensees are solely responsible and liable for all music clearances and shall indemnify the copyright owners of the play(s) and their licensing agent, Samuel French, against any costs, expenses, losses and liabilities arising from the use of music by licensees. Please contact the appropriate music licensing authority in your territory for the rights to any incidental music.

IMPORTANT BILLING AND CREDIT REQUIREMENTS

If you have obtained performance rights to this title, please refer to your licensing agreement for important billing and credit requirements.

MMF was first presented as part of the New York International Fringe Festival on August 10, 2014 by Goldfish Memory Productions and Catie Humphreys. The director was David Kimple; the lighting was by Maxwell Bowman; the sound was by Dan Spitaliere; the stage manager was Andrea Miller. The cast was as follows:

DEAN. . . . . Michael Mizwicki

JANE . . . . .Courtney Alana Ward

MICHAEL . . . . .Andrew Rincón

CHARACTERS

DEAN – Male. Any ethnicity. The young version of a man in his mid-late twenties trying to figure himself out.

JANE – Female. Any ethnicity. The same age as Dean but stands in the strength of her womanhood.

MICHAEL – Male. Any ethnicity. Somehow a bit more of a grown-up than his partners.

TIME

Present day.

AUTHOR'S NOTES

(—) indicates a shift that could, perhaps, be defined as a scene change or a beat change but should never be defined with a blackout.

(–) before or after dialogue indicates a line being interrupted; lines do not overlap.

There is no intermission.

ACKNOWLEDGMENTS

Special thank you to Courtney, Catie, Elizabeth, Blaine, Stephanie, Mark, Giselle, Emmeline, Lauren, Sammy, Denise and Greg, and my Fam.

"If I'd had the moon, if love were enough,
all might have been different."

– *Albert Camus, "Caligula"*

(DEAN, wearing yesterday's jeans and t-shirt, hurries into the room. MICHAEL and JANE follow, preparing for the day. MICHAEL grabs his belongings and JANE hers.)

JANE. Okay. Coffee, bagel, purse, Chapstick. What else?

MICHAEL. Shoes. Why are we always late?

JANE. It's Dean's fault.

MICHAEL. Cuddlemonster.

JANE. Never on time in the winter.

DEAN. I don't like being cold. I like to stay in the sheets.

MICHAEL. And when you're in the middle you cling like a koala.

(They embrace for a moment of stillness.)

JANE. I've gotta go or I'm going to have to take a cab.

MICHAEL. Take a cab. You deserve it.

JANE. Oh my god. Thank you!

DEAN. Can I take a cab?

MICHAEL. You don't have to be in until noon. You can hike. Okay.
Train time. Love you.

(They all kiss. There is a system.)

DEAN. Love you.

JANE. Love you!

(JANE grabs MICHAEL's hand and pulls him out the door. JANE's voice trails off as they exit.)

Ride with me as low as Columbus Circle then I'll keep going –

(DEAN holds a martini.)

DEAN. You know, this is my fifth martini. I'm not exactly sure how many martinis is a lot of martinis, but this is my fifth martinis. Martini.

(He sips and shudders with disgust.)

Okay. I'm lying. It's my first and I can't drink it. I really hate vodka. Vodka. VODka. VodKa.

Like it's trying to gnaw at something. Not like bourbon, for instance. *(He instructs.)* Bourrrrbon. Vodka. Bourbon. Vodka. Potato Vodka. Potatoes in my glass.

(He slams the martini down his throat.)

I'm being ridiculous today because I miss someone that I'm not allowed to miss. I'm not supposed to miss them and so I am indulging in my ridiculousness. I don't need permission.

I need to flesh a few things out. Get a few thi... Flesh things? Is it Flesh? Flesh things out? Flush? So I can Flush things out? No matter.

From the beginning.

I've just gotten out of a relationship. My relationship has just ended. I was just in a thing and now I'm not in that thing. I got dumped.

Years ago I met a boy.

—

*(Perhaps **MICHAEL** appears.)*

I'm on an airplane and I see this guy with these immaculately folded sleeves. He's checking his ticket. He sits in my row. I'm at the window and he sits on the aisle. Of course we acknowledge one another, but there isn't any conversation. It was immediate energetic tension. That sizzle. Like adding texture into open space. And then this sixteen-year-old girl sits between us. She's chubby. Go figure.

I can't stop noticing him – he smells clean. Fucking Dior.

At some point during the flight I end up having to use the bathroom. I alert the team. As I'm getting up I slip and end up plopping onto perfect-sleeve-guy's knee. (Only for a second though.) Rebounded out of that scenario more quickly than I knew my body was capable of. I come back and we are sitting next to each other.

MICHAEL. I wanted to be closer to the window.

DEAN. We were sitting next to each other and our knees kept touching.

—

MICHAEL. Hi.

DEAN. *(He giggles.)* Sorry. Hi.

    (He giggles.)

I don't typically think of myself as a giggler.

MICHAEL. You are definitely a giggler.

    (They giggle.)

—

DEAN. In retrospect, I can't help but laugh when I think about how much of a doof I was. Knowing him now, I mean. We've talked about this whole thing a million times. We love it, actually. I love it. He's not much for sentiment.

    (**JANE** *breaks in with groceries.*)

—

JANE. Cereal, Milk, Hummus, Toast –

DEAN. Bread –

JANE. Don't correct me, I know it's bread before it's toast –

DEAN. You always say –

JANE. Don't care.

DEAN. – to correct you.

JANE. I take it back every time!

DEAN. I pretend not to hear you.

JANE. I got you carob chips.

DEAN. I'm sorry?

JANE. Carob chips. They're supposed to taste like chocolate.

DEAN. Why didn't you just buy me chocolate?

JANE. You said you wanted to eat better, didn't you? Christ, Deany, you're really driving me nuts lately. Woof, I have to pee!

(JANE *makes a beeline across the room with the groceries and remains offstage for the next few lines.*)

DEAN. Sorry!

JANE. Whatever.

DEAN. My metabolism can handle a little chocolate.

JANE. You're the one who complains about being too skinny all the damn time.

DEAN. I should eat more chocolate.

JANE. I'm just trying to help.

DEAN. You're right.

JANE. Because you asked me to. Don't come in I'm peeing.

DEAN. Still on the couch. Thanks.

JANE. If you don't want to eat well and get some exercise and –

DEAN. Okay. Thanks.

(JANE *re-enters.*)

JANE. When was the last time you went to the gym?

DEAN. Yesterday morning.

JANE. Really?

DEAN. Yeah.

JANE. But –

DEAN. But what?

JANE. There must be some qualifier.

DEAN. Not really.

JANE. But – you went to the bar last night. But you forgot to eat for the rest of the day. But –

DEAN. Point taken. Dean needs to take care of himself better.

JANE. Yes.

DEAN. Yes.

JANE. I push you because you asked me too.

DEAN. You're right, coach.

JANE. If your mother – if she were here she'd walk through the kitchen and say the same things that I do.

DEAN. I eat healthily enough just not enough. You don't know my mother.

JANE. You don't eat enough and when you do eat the food is shit. Sugar, cereal, soda, yada yada. I've proved my point.

DEAN. I'm not convinced.

JANE. That's because you know you've lost.

DEAN. No. I win.

JANE. Really? Really? You want to go there – okay. Okay. Okay!

> (JANE *leaves and we hear shuffling through the cupboards of the kitchen.*)

(offstage) Moon-pies?

DEAN. Oh my god.

JANE. Bananas –

DEAN. SEE! Fruit!

JANE. No. Bananas and cream flavored 'Sinful Creations.' "Love in your mouth." Ew.

DEAN. That's not mine?

JANE. Oh my god.

DEAN. What?

JANE. Oh my god.

DEAN. What?

> (JANE *re-enters with a box of cereal.*)

JANE. Captain Munchies?

DEAN. Uh Oh.

JANE. Captain Munchies?

DEAN. They're delicious.

JANE. When you're five.

DEAN. I like them five. Fine. You like them too!

JANE. I do not.

DEAN. Yes you do. I've seen you eat an entire box.

JANE. When I was hung over. Shut up. That doesn't mean I like them.

DEAN. And those munchies saved the day.

JANE. Okay, in that instance maybe, yeah, okay, they did. That one time. They did. So, but –

DEAN. *(in a mock 'commercial' voice)* Captain Munchies: Hangover cure of the year since 1957.

JANE. This batch was probably made in '57. These things are gross. Cardboard in your bowl.

DEAN. Potatoes in my glass.

JANE. Vile.

DEAN. They cut the roof of my mouth and I love them.

JANE. You know what? We're getting rid of the munchies.

DEAN. No you're not!

JANE. Yep. I'm dumping the munchies! We're going full-on kitchen makeover up in here.

DEAN. No. Give them to me. I'll eat them right now.

JANE. No!

> *(They fight over the cereal and* JANE *runs off to the kitchen.* DEAN *jumps up and chases her immediately. The room is empty now but we can hear a flirtatious and giggle-filled battle happening in the next room. After a moment of this,* DEAN *comes back in with the box of cereal while* JANE's *voice remains offstage.)*

This isn't over!

DEAN. Cereal. Boom.

—

DEAN. I dreamt you came back and we were together and, despite your stubble, your skin was the softest thing I'd ever felt. I woke up lonely and wondering why I'd ever let my guard down long enough to find hope for us. Even in my dreams. You're one of those people that I will always want. You're one of those impossible men.

The first time I saw you, that very second, I knew I would love you. It makes it harder that I knew you would love me too.

MICHAEL. The timing isn't right. I don't think the timing will ever be quite right for us, actually. I'm thiry-one and I want a baby.

DEAN. In addition to other things, I just don't think I have the hips for child birth.

—

MICHAEL. I'm Michael.

DEAN. Dean. Nice to meet you. Sorry I fell on you.

MICHAEL. Oh, it's quite alright. So. Where you headed, Dean?

DEAN. He was asking me questions and I was answering and I was talking to this complete stranger. And I didn't even know him.

MICHAEL. You have to get to know people before you know people.

DEAN. So, what? What is the point?

—

Maybe I don't know what being in love is like. Or I didn't. Or I don't. I don't know. Maybe no one actually knows what being in love is like. Because when everyone thinks that they're in love it is actually infatuation and some people might say that love and infatuation are not mutually inclusive.

This is what I know. I have had feelings. I have feelings now that are making me think that maybe I'm in love with her, but maybe not. I think I just can't have what

I want and that is frustrating. Or the impossibility of
it all seems so luxurious or decadent or malevolent or
multi-syllabic or something.

The difference. Michael made me nervous. Like really
nervous. Sick, actually. Sometimes around him I'd get
stomachaches and headaches. He thinks I'm allergic
to him.

One day we're on a bench by the East River.

—

MICHAEL. I have something I want to say.

DEAN. This was a turning point in our relationship, I think.
I know. I think. It was. Definite point of turning.

MICHAEL. I have a crush on you.

DEAN. And I said –

> *(Stares at* **MICHAEL** *silently for too long;* **DEAN**
> *does not know what to say.)*

Which was a terrible idea! I think now if I had said
something like "I think I have a crush on you too," that
would have been much better.

MICHAEL. I feel bad for saying anything because I know
that you don't feel the same way but I feel like I like you
and I'm embarrassed and won't bother you anymore.

DEAN. My dumb ass is sitting there letting him macerate
himself. I grabbed him and sat him down. I looked him
dead in the face and didn't really say anything (idiot)
but just –

> **(DEAN** *smirks,* **MICHAEL** *smiles, they both accept
> that they feel the same.)*

—

JANE. *(offstage)* Why is there water all over the floor?

DEAN. What?

JANE. Water – why is it wet?

DEAN. Why is water wet?

JANE. Have you been drinking?

DEAN. Oh, that. I had a drink, yeah. I sort of dropped it.

JANE. Well, why didn't you clean it up?

DEAN. I don't know.

JANE. Cool. I'll clean it up. I love cleaning up your messes.

> (*We see* JANE *wiping the floor while they talk. She is mostly just popping in and out, never really entering the room. An arm. Gone. The top of her head. Gone. Arm. Head.*)

DEAN. Oh, Cinderelly, you look marvelous.

JANE. Fuck off okay?

DEAN. Okay.

JANE. Okay. Oh! Hey. We need to figure out the plan for tomorrow.

DEAN. Tomorrow?

JANE. Yeah. What's the deal?

DEAN. Um –

JANE. What?

DEAN. What is –

JANE. Oh no. Dean, please don't flake. I don't want to have to make excuses. It's been a long couple of days. The store is a friggin' mess and –

DEAN. Not flaking. Flake free. Head and Shoulders. Just a little confused.

JANE. With tomorrow night? You coming or are you making me do this alone?

DEAN. What am I missing?

> (JANE *fully enters the room.*)

JANE. Jesus. Mee-Maw. Pop-Pop. They're here. They want to meet my – my – my – you. My whatever you are. My you.

DEAN. Your you. Me. Your me. ME. They want to meet me. Dean.

JANE. Why wouldn't they?

DEAN. What?

JANE. Why wouldn't they want to meet you?

DEAN. I'm a little –

JANE. You're Dean. I Talk About "Dean" all the time to them. Two times a week-ish, we're chatting, we're avoiding politics, updates about Mom's new boobs, –

DEAN. Owooga!

JANE. – and Dean things.

DEAN. Dean things.

JANE. Yes. Is that honestly such a shock to you?

DEAN. I guess so. I didn't really realize –

JANE. What?

DEAN. That we were talking about each other to family?

JANE. Hold on –

DEAN. You're upset –

JANE. – you haven't –

DEAN. But don't be upset because –

JANE. – told any of your family about us?

DEAN. I have, but –

JANE. BUT? How is that possible? Things changed, Dean. The rules –

DEAN. Changed. The rules changed. They just don't know the details, if you will.

JANE. Oh.

DEAN. No explicit details.

JANE. Oh.

DEAN. Yeah.

JANE. Oh.

DEAN. Yeah.

JANE. Well, but, so, but, um, –

DEAN. Yeah.

JANE. Still?

DEAN. It's –

JANE. Why exactly is that?

DEAN. I don't really know what to tell them.

JANE. Oh.

DEAN. Yeah.

JANE. It's a bit –

DEAN. It's a bit something. That's for sure.

JANE. Okay.

DEAN. Yeah. How we met.

JANE. What do you tell them?

DEAN. What?

JANE. When they ask you about your love life?

DEAN. I don't know.

JANE. How don't you know?

DEAN. I'm not trying to hide you, I just haven't –

JANE. I'm like your sweet roomie.

DEAN. No.

JANE. Okay. You know what, it's okay, Dean.

DEAN. Really?

JANE. I've taken a breath. This isn't about me. It's about you. It's okay. Really.

DEAN. Really really or just really like you're kind of upset or mad but you –

JANE. I'm fine. It's fine. It's not about me.

DEAN. And you're not bottling a feeling for later?

JANE. Dean, I get it. Can we move on?!

DEAN. Um. Yeah. Let's go.

JANE. Okay. Barring any explicit details, Mee-Maw and Pop-Pop still think you're someone worth sizing up.

DEAN. Of course.

JANE. Wear a collar.

DEAN. I love a sensible collar. You say it as if I wouldn't wear something nice.

JANE. From the man wearing one sock. I just don't want it to be weird.

DEAN. Well as long as they don't ask us how we met.

JANE. Har Har.

DEAN. But really.

JANE. I know.

DEAN. Maybe we should make a game plan.

>(JANE *grabs the wet towel off the floor and walks out.*)

—

>(DEAN *sits in silence for a moment, staring at the ceiling. He shares a moment in silence with* MICHAEL *but before they make it to words –*)

JANE. *(offstage)* Dean, come here.

—

DEAN. Why?

JANE. I don't know.

DEAN. Why don't you just talk to me in here?!

JANE. *(offstage)* Just c'mere.

DEAN. What, weirdo?

>(JANE *enters. She has changed into* DEAN*'s sweatshirt.*)

JANE. Whatcha doin?

DEAN. What are you wearing?

JANE. Nothing.

DEAN. Something. My favorite sweatshirt.

JANE. So. I can wear it. It's my favorite.

DEAN. Yes. You're very cute.

>(DEAN *and* JANE *are on the couch together flirting like every couple you've ever hated.*)

JANE. Am I?

DEAN. Very cute.

JANE. Wouldn't you like me to take it off?

DEAN. Maybe I would.

JANE. Maybe I will – not. I'm cold.

DEAN. Tease.

JANE. You love it.

DEAN. I might.

JANE. You do.

DEAN. I might.

JANE. You do.

(They almost connect. DEAN *slips away.)*

So what's going on here? What are you doing? You're tossing drinks around the apartment for me to clean up, not eating the food I buy, and sitting? Sitting on the couch? No book. No TV. Not a thing. Hm?

DEAN. There is a thing.

JANE. What thing?

DEAN. I'm just thinking. That's all.

JANE. Thinking?

DEAN. Yeah.

JANE. What?

DEAN. I don't really –

JANE. What?

DEAN. – want to talk about it.

JANE. Oh.

DEAN. It's no big deal.

JANE. Gotcha.

DEAN. Don't worry. I just don't want to talk about it right now.

JANE. Just think about it?

DEAN. Sort of.

JANE. Well, will you tell me whatever it is later?

DEAN. Yeah, yeah.

JANE. Cool. Then we're good.

DEAN. Yup.

JANE. Can we watch TV?

DEAN. Um.

JANE. What?

DEAN. Nothing.

JANE. What?

DEAN. Nothing. Sure, TV. Sure.

JANE. No, what? That was your Um-thing. What's up?

DEAN. Just. Can we just not watch TV? Can you watch TV in the bedroom and I'll sit out here for just a little bit longer?

JANE. Oh. Yeah. I guess. I mean. But, um, but –

DEAN. I'm fine, I promise. I'm just trying to flush a few things out.

JANE. Okay.

Is it me?

DEAN. No.

JANE. Are you sure?

DEAN. Kind of. I'm just not there yet.

JANE. Well, is there something I can do?

DEAN. Not really.

JANE. Is it something I did?

DEAN. Sort of –

JANE. Oh.

DEAN. – but don't worry about it. Give me a minute.

JANE. Okay.

(She starts leaving but stops short.)

Can I have a kiss?

(DEAN rises and gives her a kiss. JANE exits.)

DEAN. Jane is – something. This gorgeous, magnetic, individual person. We'd both be lying to ourselves if we said that our relationship is easy. It's not easy. It's really hard. We don't exactly know how to be together yet. We don't know how to be together without –

Michael met her one day on his way to the office.

——

JANE. You know, I debated coming over here, but I wanted to tell you that your boyfriend and you are a very handsome couple.

MICHAEL. Oh. Thank you – but he isn't really my boyfriend.

JANE. Oh really?

MICHAEL. We're probably not sleeping with anyone else – I'm not – but he's not my boyfriend. It's only been a couple of weeks. He's my notboyfriend.

JANE. You're funny. Let's grab coffee. Coffee cart. Five minutes. I'm Jane.

—

DEAN. The first time the three of us hung out, we went to dinner and laughed and drank and had a really really great time.

There is energy between the three of us. Incomparable.

MICHAEL. Something about her just –

JANE. We buzz. That night, you guys are at Dean's place having an extra glass of wine and talk about me. I love this story. For two hours.

DEAN. Everything about you

MICHAEL. and the things you say

DEAN. and the things she thought

MICHAEL. and the way she moves

DEAN. and the way she dresses and wears her hair and jewelry.

MICHAEL. Her strength. She has this natural strength about her that isn't forced or manufactured. She didn't develop it because of a hard childhood or anything.

DEAN. Just strong. This steel core.

—

Do you like her? I think I like her.

MICHAEL. You're attracted to her.

DEAN. Yes.

MICHAEL. Me too.

—

DEAN. And the next thing I know we are together for two years.

JANE. Almost.

DEAN. Three people who are attracted to each other equally and care equally and want to be together. There is Jane to finish my thoughts

MICHAEL. and you to finish mine

JANE. and Michael to tell us what we think and when we think it and we just ping-pong, boopbooped and zip-zapped ourselves into this private, perfect little world.

MICHAEL. It is never strange.

DEAN. We just work. It just worked. Except it didn't work.

—

Jane, I love you. You know? I do love you. But, what Michael and I have is something else.

MICHAEL. Had. Because we don't have it anymore, do we?

DEAN. No we don't.

—

JANE. It might seem odd, but I don't find it surprising that you're going through a period of loneliness.
Transitional phases tend to do that to people.

DEAN. Excuse me?

JANE. Things changed recently. So you're freaking out. You're going through this thing. This feeling like the world is off hilter.

DEAN. Kilter.

JANE. It doesn't feel right, right?

DEAN. No it doesn't, doesn't.

JANE. It's not like we've been left all alone. Babe. I've got you, babe.

DEAN. Right.

JANE. I have been stuck about what is happening with us. I have this new found inability to understand what you need from me. You, Dean. The one person I've always been on the same plane as. Who knows, maybe it's always been you and me –

DEAN. What?

JANE. We've always matched a little bit more anyway.

DEAN. Yeah. I don't know.

JANE. What are you 'thinking' about?

DEAN. What?

JANE. We've got to start somewhere. What are you thinking about? Share with me or something, because I can't read your mind. All I see is this tired, emotional man sitting on my couch slamming vodka down his throat.

DEAN. It's my couch, really.

JANE. I sit on it too.

DEAN. So.

JANE. So?

DEAN. I don't know what to say.

JANE. Great. We'll just sit here then. Stare at the walls and get drunk on my vodka. Yes. "We'll sit in silence for a minute and the air feels thin and we're lost in our own skin."

DEAN. Don't mock me.

JANE. What?

DEAN. I don't know.

JANE. Yeah. – Try?

DEAN. I guess I've been thinking about – these – No. Yeah. These – all of these things we endure in our young lives. The feelings. Road blocks or stepping stones.

JANE. Transitions.

DEAN. I feel so much. So many things all at the same time that it is like I'll never make it out alive.

Sometimes I honestly don't think I can handle being inside my own head anymore, like I'm not going to make it to see another day but, realistically, isn't this all just preparation for later? If we do make it to thirty years old. Or forty. Fifty. We are going to need this immunity. We feel everything so intensely right now because it has never happened to us before. Next time we'll understand why it hurts and that deafens the pain. The next time it will be less and again and again. Eventually we might not even notice the things that torment us right now. We're being immunized for life.

JANE. Either way, perhaps next time we'll be all right.

DEAN. Perhaps.

JANE. You know, you're not actually telling me how or why you're having feelings.

DEAN. Okay.

JANE. You're doing that thing you always do.

DEAN. I love that song.

JANE. Stop. That's it. Stop avoiding me. You understand it better than you're letting on.

DEAN. I just told you –

JANE. You told me something.

DEAN. Yes.

JANE. But that something isn't it.

DEAN. Okay.

JANE. You have on this mask of profound bullshit that sounds just dandy, but you're not actually making any sense. You're not actually saying what you mean. You're not actually saying anything.

DEAN. How do you know?

JANE. – Why did Michael leave us?

DEAN. What?

JANE. Why did he leave us?

DEAN. Michael?

JANE. Yeah. Michael.

DEAN. Really?

JANE. Michael. I finally said it.

DEAN. You did.

JANE. It's out there. Why did Michael leave us?

DEAN. I don't know. That's not the –

JANE. The what?

DEAN. The point.

JANE. The point?

DEAN. Yeah.

JANE. Then what is, Dean?

DEAN. I don't know.

JANE. Come on.

DEAN. I think I'm just bored in the world.

JANE. No no. That's another excuse. That's another way for you to justify being moody. A way to 'explain' yourself without actually –

DEAN. He told you that he just couldn't do it anymore, didn't he?

JANE. That's what he said, but I don't believe him. I mean, yes I believe that he couldn't do it anymore, but I don't believe it's as simple as him tiring of it.
Tiring of us.

DEAN. What else could it be?

JANE. What happened?

DEAN. Nothing.

JANE. Not nothing. What happened?

DEAN. Nothing. No thing.

JANE. Don't coddle me. And stop talking to me like I don't know when you're lying. Stop.

DEAN. Okay.

JANE. I'm just too tired of it all.

DEAN. Okay.

JANE. Just tired.

DEAN. Okay.

JANE. Tired of knowing that I don't know something.

DEAN. Okay.

JANE. Okay?

DEAN. Yes. Okay.

JANE. You're going to talk to me?

DEAN. Yes.

JANE. About Michael?

DEAN. About us.

JANE. Us and Michael too?

DEAN. Yes, but –

JANE. No but –

DEAN. Yes, but. Look, if we're talking about this, like really talking about this, then you have to listen to me and know something. First of all, I love you. Do you hear me? I love you. Take the time and hear that before we have this –

JANE. Okay. I hear you.

DEAN. These last few months, having been with you and only you, I feel like I love you.

JANE. Okay…but?

DEAN. Something happened.

JANE. Mmhmm.

DEAN. I did something.

JANE. Something. Something?

DEAN. I did a thing.

JANE. A something. My throat just got all burny. A what thing?

DEAN. A while back –

JANE. Before he left us –

DEAN. I asked Michael to be with me.

JANE. What?

DEAN. And only me.

(JANE *stands and stops.*)

Wait, just stop for a minute. Don't panic or be upset. Just hear me out for a minute. Okay?

JANE. You did what? No. Absolutely not.

DEAN. Look. Look at me for one second, Janey.

JANE. Oh my god.

DEAN. I asked him –

JANE. What? When?

DEAN. I was feeling –

JANE. Always feeling –

DEAN. It's not the same anymore though.

JANE. Oh my god.

DEAN. It's not the same anymore though.

JANE. Sure isn't.

DEAN. I mean that I'm good now.

JANE. You're good now? You were bad before?

DEAN. I thought I needed him –

JANE. Right. And not me.

DEAN. He left.

JANE. And not me!

DEAN. Yes.

JANE. You asked him –

DEAN. Right.

JANE. But not me.

DEAN. It was a while back.

JANE. I know that part.

DEAN. I thought I needed him and he left.

JANE. And we stayed.

DEAN. Right.

JANE. You wanted to be with him and he said no and so you stayed with me just because?

DEAN. Not just because.

JANE. I'm missing the transition!

DEAN. I thought I needed him –

JANE. This we have established. WHY? What changed?

DEAN. But I don't. Well, I don't want to.

JANE. Want? Present tense?

DEAN. I'm just – It's not – It's –

JANE. You're floundering.

DEAN. I'm trying –

JANE. I think I'm going to throw up.

DEAN. You're not going to throw up.

JANE. Don't try and tell me what I'm doing.

DEAN. You're panicking

JANE. You're not helping.

DEAN. What am I supposed to say?

JANE. Something.

DEAN. Okay.

JANE. Just start talking, Dean!

DEAN. It's scary to imagine that, seemingly without warning, someone you invest yourself in can just flip flop and leave you in the dark. Isn't it? Just imagine. Right now you're sitting next to a person that you share everything with.

JANE. I am –

DEAN. You let them use your car or see you naked or cook you dinner. They tell you that they love you and you just beam. There is no greater feeling in the entire world than that moment where it feels like the two of you are on the same page. Having the same feelings. It feels like it could really work. It could really be real. Tomorrow they're going to tell you that they don't love you and you're not the most important thing anymore and maybe you never were.

JANE. What are you saying?

DEAN. Did I make up how great it was sometimes? I mean, of course it was never perfect. But sometimes wasn't it just – perfect? It was, I think. The first time we slept together. He spent the night. That's not in the rule book. It's not. You're supposed to leave afterward and go home alone. He stayed and the next morning, when he was leaving my apartment we kissed a kiss that was inappropriately familiar. It shouldn't have made as much sense as it did but it did and then he closed the door. Two seconds go by and the door flies open again. He walks back inside and kisses me one more time.

This perfect euphoric kiss. Giddy and familiar kisses that make me beam. Wasn't that perfect? Wasn't it? How could I remember something so specifically and so fondly and it not be perfect?

Well, he was never one for details and I'm terrified. Terrified that I will forever be hung up on a boy that's not in my life anymore. Hasn't been in forever and he is the only one I've known that knots me up like this. I seriously can't take it. I can't handle how terrible it makes me feel that I can be laying in bed next to a perfectly great girl but still – wish she was someone else. Someone that debatably knows my name anymore. It's ludicrous and embarrassing and I just want it to stop. I want it to stop. I want him to not be around and not to know the people I know and not text me "Good Luck" or "I miss you." But if he doesn't say Good Luck and eventually come over for drinks and light up just a little if he sees me in the street, if he doesn't do that. I'll – Wow.

What the fuck is wrong with me? He means nothing. He's no one. He isn't anything. He's an idea. A theory. A trinket. I'm losing it. I'm losing it. And I haven't talked this out with anyone yet. Because I can't. I'm too embarrassed. But I needed someone and I'm sorry.

JANE. Right.

DEAN. I love you, though.

JANE. Okay.

DEAN. Okay.

JANE. Okay.

DEAN. What?

JANE. What?

DEAN. Why aren't you saying anything?

JANE. Because you're not saying anything.

DEAN. What?

JANE. What?

DEAN. What?

JANE. What?

DEAN. What? I just don't know what to say right now.

JANE. And what, my dear, would you like me to say?

DEAN. Um –

JANE. You want me to tell you the essence of this whole thing? This is the point, Deany. You've just, oh my god, you've just turned me into you. You sit here telling me that you love me and allow me to believe that you and I are the ones with that extra little spark. The thing that will keep us going beyond Michael. Beyond the bullshit. Beyond the pale or whatever. You've let me believe that there was something we could salvage in this relationship from that relationship when, in reality, you don't actually want it. How could you want to be with me and only me when, at some point, you wanted to get rid of me altogether?

DEAN. It's not that I wanted to get rid – I don't want to get rid –

JANE. Then what did you want to do? Bullshit.

DEAN. I didn't try and do anything maliciously.

JANE. You just used me.

DEAN. No.

JANE. Yes. Yes you didn't think about me. You just found me. You happened upon another warm body to pass the time with.

DEAN. I'm not lying when I say that I love you.

JANE. Okay! I believe that you love me. I believe you. You just don't care about me.

DEAN. I do.

JANE. God! You're so selfish.

Dean, I've loved you as wholly as I possibly could from the first day that I met you. I loved Michael as much as I possibly could from the day I met him. The three of us, we fucking worked and then there was that one day where Michael is gone because he 'can't do it anymore' and my heart drops to the floor.

He left me too dammit.

It hasn't been good since he left, I know that, but I have worked my ass off to not be heartbroken and damaged and to just be with you and love you and deal with you – you and your roundabout bullshit – because I know that this has been hard on both of us.

DEAN. It's just that I've become this person –

JANE. I don't care, Dean! I don't. I'm sick and tired of listening to your self-analysis and justifications.

You're an emotional little boy and you probably always will be. That said, even little boys know what they're doing when they're hiding. When they're lying. When they're breaking things to pieces.

DEAN. What do you want from me right now?

JANE. Honesty. Unfiltered honesty. Don't sugarcoat.

DEAN. I'm trying.

JANE. Not hard enough.

(*There is a moment.*)

DEAN. I'm afraid of hurting you.

JANE. You're afraid of hurting me?

DEAN. Yes.

JANE. That is the most arrogant thing I've ever heard.

DEAN. What?

JANE. You think you can hurt me? You assume that you have enough power over me to hurt me.

DEAN. What is the point of being honest if the person you're being honest with is going call you arrogant for trying to do the right thing?

JANE. You're not hurting me. You're pissing me off. Yeah. No. You didn't hurt me, Dean. But you sure as shit left a scar. A nice shiny scar visible to everyone – and no one – and oh my god – I'm starting to talk like you.

DEAN. Is that supposed to be some sort of insult?

JANE. YES.

Yeah. I'll see you later.

DEAN. Okay.

JANE. No. I deserve more than that. Than this. I'm having this moment right now where I feel like I'm not supposed to ask questions. Like I did something wrong. Guilty. Why? I didn't – oh my god. I need more than this, Dean.

>   (**JANE** *leaves.*)

>   —

DEAN. I don't feel well. My throat is twisting around.

>   (**DEAN** *makes a phone call.*)

Michael? Hi. You answered.

Don't be mad at me anymore, okay? I don't want you to be mad at me. Don't be mad at me.

Come over.

MICHAEL. He doesn't know what to do with his body.

DEAN. I don't know what to do with my body.

>   (**DEAN** *exits.*)

>   —

>   (**MICHAEL** *begins to enter.*)

MICHAEL. Dean?

Dean?

Jane?

>   (**MICHAEL** *is alone in the space for a significant amount of time. He goes into another room and returns. He catches himself holding a duffle bag and letter.*)

What am I doing?

>   (**JANE** *enters.*)

>   —

JANE. Okay. Let's okay. Listen we'll –

JANE.	**MICHAEL.**
Michael!	Jane.

MICHAEL. I just walked in –

JANE. Hi.

MICHAEL. The door was open, so I just –

JANE. Hi.

MICHAEL. I didn't know you were going to –

JANE. Hi. I said hi. Hi, Michael. Hi.

MICHAEL. Jane. What's going on?

JANE. Well –

MICHAEL. What?

JANE. Don't interrupt me, Michael!

MICHAEL. Whoa.

JANE. I'm trying to tell you.
    Hi. First, hi. Wowzie. It's been a little while and I think that's most appropriate. To say 'Hi' to someone you love.

MICHAEL. Okay. Hi. Hi, Jane. Hi.

JANE. Thank you.

MICHAEL. Sure.

JANE. Wow.

MICHAEL. Hi.

JANE. You know you've got a little bit of a drawl sometimes. Especially when you say things like "Hi." And, for whatever reason, when I hear your voice in my head, like if I'm remembering something that you said or if I'm imagining what you would say, I remember everything you say with that little twang.

MICHAEL. Okay.

JANE. You look wonderful.

MICHAEL. Thanks –

JANE. Stunning.

MICHAEL. Jane.

JANE. Michael.

> (JANE *moves to* MICHAEL *and hugs him hard. There is love. It is mutually romantic in some capacity.*)

MICHAEL. Hi, Janey.

> (JANE *holds on a little longer. They almost connect.*
> MICHAEL *slips away.*)

MICHAEL. Okay. Jane, come on –
   Wow. It's really you.

JANE. In the goofy flesh.

MICHAEL. My heart is beating.

JANE. That's a relief.

MICHAEL. Hard.

JANE. Pounding.

MICHAEL. Yes. It's really good to see you.

JANE. I'm glad you're here.

MICHAEL. Okay.

JANE. Okay –

MICHAEL. – enough pandering.

JANE. You smell good. Pandering? Is that the right word?

MICHAEL. Yes. What?

JANE. What?

MICHAEL. You sound like Dean.

JANE. He turned me into him.

MICHAEL. Okay. Well. Now what?

JANE. What?

MICHAEL. What?

JANE. Dean told me.

MICHAEL. What did he tell you?

JANE. Everything.

MICHAEL. What is –

JANE. I just want you to know that I know. I know what
   happened and now we can start over.

MICHAEL. Start over?

JANE. Yes. Reset button. And if he doesn't want to then
   maybe just you and I could –

MICHAEL. I don't think it's so simple as that.

JANE. But it is. It is so simple. All we have to do is say that we love each other and start over. I'm here and you're here, right? You're here out of the blue so we just start trying again, you know? Start trying to get back to – to back to before. Get back there.

MICHAEL. Jane.

JANE. Michael, please.

MICHAEL. Where is Dean?

JANE. Where is Dean?

MICHAEL. Where is Dean? Yes. He's not here.

JANE. He's not here?

MICHAEL. He's not here. I didn't see him anywhere.

JANE. I left him here.

MICHAEL. You don't know where he is?

JANE. What are you doing here?

MICHAEL. What?

JANE. What are you doing here?

MICHAEL. Dean.

JANE. What?

MICHAEL. Dean.

JANE. Dean what?

MICHAEL. Called.

JANE. You?

MICHAEL. Mmhmm.

JANE. And asked you to meet him here?

MICHAEL. Yeah…

JANE. Right.

MICHAEL. Are you okay?

JANE. Why?

MICHAEL. Jane.

JANE. What?

MICHAEL. Are you okay?

JANE. I'm fine. I'm buzzing. I've just drunk about two pints of Manhattans.

MICHAEL. Explanations for the mania.

JANE. This is good.

MICHAEL. Is it?

JANE. This is a good thing. I think we should all be in the same place because something has to happen now. I'm tired of this retrospection and regurgitation. The rehashing is pissing me off.

MICHAEL. Rehashing?

JANE. It's like we're always talking about something that happened before. Dwelling on the past.

MICHAEL. Well the past can be pertinent –

JANE. – at times, but not now. Now I think that the three of us, we, we need to be in the now right now and say THIS IS HOW I FEEL RIGHT NOW.

MICHAEL. Have you been staying with Dean this whole time?

JANE. You didn't know?

MICHAEL. I guessed, but how would I know?

JANE. I left messages.

MICHAEL. I deleted them.

JANE. You deleted my messages? You deleted me? You deleted me. That's lovely. Just write me off when I did nothing wrong –

MICHAEL. Don't do that.

JANE. I mean, I knew you weren't answering my calls but I never imagined that you'd just boopboop delete me.

MICHAEL. Don't.

JANE. What?

MICHAEL. Demonize me. I needed my space. I didn't want it but I needed that space so I could move on.

JANE. What?

MICHAEL. What would you have me do? Listen to your messages and call you back and have a chat about my day and my plans for the week? We know all the same people. It's awful. I can't get away from you. If I was going to keep my head above ground, I needed the space. From you.

JANE. Above water. You're making it sound like I didn't need the space too. Like I couldn't have used a moment to gather my thoughts.

MICHAEL. Of course you did –

JANE. The difference between you and me is right there. Between you and me and me and Dean and me and we – there are too many of us together in all of this – the difference is that I'm always thinking of you in tandem with me. Not before myself but at the same time. I consider all of us at the same time – you both always think of yourselves and just yourselves – it seems like you think of no one but yourselves and then you try and convince me that you were thinking of me the whole time but you weren't you were thinking of yourself – and you know what, I needed the space too, I did, but I would have at least told you that I was going to take the space instead of just making you disappear – instead of disappearing without warning.

MICHAEL. I don't care.

JANE. Nice. Real nice.

MICHAEL. No, really.

JANE. Before you left?

MICHAEL. After. I have to make myself decide not to care about what you thought. Or what Dean thought. Because if I'm going to get beyond the bullshit then I need to be able to put you aside and think about what it is that I want for myself. What do I need? How do I deal with all of this?

JANE. We all have to ask ourselves those questions.

MICHAEL. I have to stop considering you if I am going to get over this. I have to if I'm ever going to get over this.

JANE. And what I am saying is that it would have been nice to know that this is what you were doing.

MICHAEL. I see your point.

JANE. It would be nice to know anything. From either of you.

MICHAEL. Jane, I'm – I don't know.

JANE. You do though.

MICHAEL. This hasn't been easy.

JANE. No.

MICHAEL. No. Dammit, where is Dean?

DEAN. I'm right here.

    I'm here.

JANE. What the hell?

MICHAEL. You've been here? Where? Where were you?

DEAN. Just lying there. Listening. Absorbing.

JANE. Dick.

MICHAEL. Jane.

DEAN. Fun.

JANE. Har Har.

(They stare each other down.)

DEAN. Michael.

MICHAEL. Dean.

    Jane.

JANE. Michael.

    Dean.

DEAN. Jane.

(There is a moment.)

MICHAEL. Okay. I'm going to go –

JANE. Called it!

DEAN. Called it?

JANE. Thought it. Called it.

MICHAEL. What?

JANE. What?

DEAN. She's saying she knew you would try and –

JANE. I knew you'd bug-out again –

MICHAEL. You act as if I ever had a choice.

DEAN. Didn't you?

MICHAEL. No. I didn't. Because of you. Hi.

DEAN. Me?

MICHAEL. Yes. Hi, Dean.

DEAN. Me? I'm not going to just accept that we ended up in this exact position because of me and only me. That isn't fair.

JANE. You're the one who did it, Dean.

DEAN. Did what?

MICHAEL. Propose.

JANE. I'm sorry what?

DEAN. Shit.

JANE. What does that mean?

DEAN. Jane.

JANE. What does that mean "propose"?

MICHAEL. Oh my god.

DEAN. Okay, I can explain.

MICHAEL. You said he told you. Told you everything.

JANE. Not everything.

MICHAEL. Dammit, Dean.

JANE. What did you do?

MICHAEL. He proposed to me.

JANE. Marriage? You did not tell me that you proposed marriage.

DEAN. It's not that different.

JANE. It is.

DEAN. I tried.

JANE. You lied.

MICHAEL. I've got to go.

JANE. Sit down, Michael.

MICHAEL. Jane, I'm sorry.

JANE. Don't apologize.

MICHAEL. Okay. Sorry.

JANE. You proposed.

DEAN. Yeah.

JANE. Marriage.

DEAN. Yeah.

JANE. On one knee?

MICHAEL. Yeah.

JANE. How is that possible?

MICHAEL. Jane, I'm so sorry. I wouldn't have said anything – I mean wouldn't have kept it a secret –

JANE. You did.

MICHAEL. I didn't mean to hurt you.

JANE. I know. Shut up.

DEAN. Jane, –

JANE. Everyone shut up. Shut up for a second!

(They shut up.)

Jesus. You really fucked this up.

MICHAEL. I'd say so.

DEAN. It's not all my fault.

MICHAEL. Maybe we can all accept some blame.

JANE. Tell me what I did and, if I agree, I'll accept some blame. Right now I'm pretty sure that I feel like a dejected bridesmaid or some shit.

DEAN. Okay, then.

MICHAEL. You're not.

JANE. All I can think about is you in tuxedos giving me the finger at a beach wedding in Cozumel.

DEAN. You have to let me clarify.

JANE. I think it's pretty clear.

MICHAEL. He got on one knee. He gave me a ring. I was just as shocked.

JANE. You should have just said that.

DEAN. I think that my feelings have been –

JANE. Stop. No. You're about to go into some sort of philosophic explanation of why you are who you are and what it is that makes you feel the way you feel –

DEAN. – because I think that the way I approached the emotions I was having about Michael are rooted in –

JANE. Bullshit. They're rooted in bullshit.

DEAN. If you want me to explain, you're going to have to let me speak.

JANE. You can speak but your explanation isn't going to satisfy us if you go too far into the past. I don't want some Freudian-esque interpretation of Dean. I want the truth.

MICHAEL. I'd like the truth as well.

DEAN. This is where I get lost, though. The truth, to me, is an intricate web of variables that compound upon one another to make me who I am. I'm trying to show you –

JANE. You see, I'm lost already. What does that mean?!

MICHAEL.	DEAN.
Give him a minute.	Give me a minute.

JANE. *(screams at them)* AHHH!

DEAN. I am trying.

JANE. Then go.

DEAN. But I don't know exactly what I want to say.

JANE. Who gives a shit?

MICHAEL. Jane.

JANE. What?

MICHAEL. Let's not make this more snarky than it has to be.

JANE. I'm ignoring that.

MICHAEL. Great.

JANE. What, Deany, has nothing to do with this.

DEAN. The truth? Okay. I've been in love with Michael for as long as I can remember knowing him.

JANE. We both have.

DEAN. I felt like I needed to be with him.

JANE. We both do.

DEAN. And I absolutely love you, Jane, with as much of myself as I can –

JANE. – but –

DEAN. – but those loves have become two different things. There is some tiny layer of need that I have for him, for you, that exists which I don't have for you, for Jane.

MICHAEL. Then why spend so much time with both of us?

DEAN. Because I love us! The ground wasn't always so uneven. I believe there was a time when the three of us matched-pitch. I feel like you feel like I'm making that up for some reason. I'm not trying to deny our relationship as it was. I love the way we are together.

MICHAEL. And – just want to point this out – we are together.

DEAN. First time in months.

JANE. Almost kind of nice.

MICHAEL. I'm nervous.

JANE. Me too.

DEAN. I'm Dean.

MICHAEL. You're never going to stop using that one –

DEAN. Probably not.

JANE. Okay. Re-focus.

MICHAEL. Sorry.

JANE. Dean.

DEAN. Okay. I think we need different people for different reasons and different times in our lives. I think we needed each other. All of us. I don't think that I need the "us" any more. I think that what I actually want is something more solid. Something pseudo-nuclear –

MICHAEL. You're ready to settle down.

DEAN. In a way, I suppose.

MICHAEL. But that's not what we used to say.

DEAN. What?

MICHAEL. When we all started this thing. Being together as three. It kind of came from not being the classic commitment-type.

JANE. Dean, do you know what he means when he says classic?

DEAN. Yes. We all said that.

JANE. And yet you're captain of team wedding band.

DEAN. I changed.

JANE. I didn't.

MICHAEL. I don't know.

JANE. Were we not happy? I was happy.

DEAN. We were. But when I imagine the future and the things that I want some day it just isn't there.

MICHAEL. The picture in your head is different.

DEAN. Knowing that the picture changes at some point changed what I feel like I need right now.

JANE. So what am I supposed to do with that? Am I supposed to just be fine with it and move on?

MICHAEL. No one is saying that you have to do anything or feel any certain way.

DEAN. I'm just telling you what you wanted to hear.

JANE. You think that this is what I want to hear?

DEAN. The truth.

MICHAEL. It's what we said we wanted from him.

JANE. Well, ew, I take it back. I don't actually take it back but I take it back. This is not what I want to hear.

DEAN. I'm not enjoying this either.

JANE. That's like me telling you that I'm pregnant.

MICHAEL. Yeah right.

DEAN. Oh god.

JANE. What if I am?

MICHAEL. – What?

DEAN. Oh my god.

JANE. What would you do?

DEAN. Oh my god.

MICHAEL. Janey. Are you being serious?

JANE. Do you believe me?

DEAN. I don't want to.

JANE. Want. Again. Hmm. Interesting.

DEAN. Jane. Please.

JANE. Michael? What do you think?

MICHAEL. I don't know. I can't tell if this is a what-if situation or you are telling us you might be – We might be pregnant?

DEAN. Would it be we?

JANE. Would it?

DEAN. You and you and me and baby makes four. Doesn't even rhyme.

JANE. I'm pregnant, boys.

MICHAEL. –

Wait. No you're not.

DEAN. Are you?

MICHAEL. She isn't.

JANE. How do you know?

MICHAEL. You promised.

JANE. I did.

DEAN. Promised what?

JANE. That if I ever had a baby –

MICHAEL. – She'd make sure it was mine.

DEAN. Why not mine?

JANE. Would you want this baby, Dean?

DEAN. Is the baby real or not?

MICHAEL. If it were it would be mine.

DEAN. It could be. You've only been gone three months.

JANE. And four days.

MICHAEL. Jane. You can stop.

DEAN. Stop? I'm confused.

JANE. Pretending.

I'm not pregnant, dipshit.

DEAN. Oh my god.

MICHAEL. Kind of wish you were.

DEAN. How did you know? She never lies about anything.

MICHAEL. Exactly.

JANE. Right. Okay. Now that we've checked that off the list. Michael, what do you have? Anything to say or add to clear this up? Help me feel better?

MICHAEL. I'm not going to say something just to make you feel better.

JANE. Typical. You're not going to say anything.

MICHAEL. Just because I don't blurt out everything that I'm thinking the minute I think it, like you, or analyze and retro-justify, like Dean, doesn't mean that I don't have anything to say. In fact, anything I do have to say right now is not going to make you feel better.

DEAN. What, you're pregnant too?

JANE. Shut up! What, Michael?

MICHAEL. More truth.

JANE. The kind I don't like.

MICHAEL. Yes.

JANE. This should be fun. In that case, I need a – I need a moment. Please allow me to take a moment to brace. I'm going to slip into something more comfortable and get a beverage. Drinking for two now, you know? Excuse me for a minute.

> (JANE *exits.* MICHAEL *and* DEAN *find themselves alone together.*)

DEAN. Hey, stranger.

MICHAEL. Hi.

DEAN. Look, I'm sorry about all of –

MICHAEL. Don't. Let's not have that moment.

DEAN. I feel bad –

MICHAEL. Okay.

DEAN. – so I just want you to know.

MICHAEL. Okay.

DEAN. Sorry.

MICHAEL. Okay.

DEAN. Are you still working?

MICHAEL. Am I still working? Dean, I moved out I didn't become a recluse and abandon society.

DEAN. Yeah.

MICHAEL. I'm pretty much in charge of all media communication.

You'd be amazed at the politicians we deal with.

DEAN. You don't have to fluff it for me.

MICHAEL. I know. I'm not.

DEAN. Okay.

MICHAEL. I thought you wanted to know.

DEAN. I do. I do. Sorry.

MICHAEL. Anyway I'm okay.

DEAN. I'm sure.

MICHAEL. But that's enough of me. How's you? How is your thing?

DEAN. My...thing?

MICHAEL. Yeah.

DEAN. You want to know about my thing?

MICHAEL. Dean.

DEAN. Oh come on, you couldn't have forgotten it entirely.

MICHAEL. I'm not talking about what's in your pants.

DEAN. Mmhmm.

MICHAEL. I'm not.

DEAN. Aw, you're blushing. My blushing boy –

MICHAEL. I am not. Stop.

DEAN. There it is.

MICHAEL. What?

DEAN. My favorite thing about your head. The smile. And the beard.

MICHAEL. Dean.

DEAN. And the puppy-dog brown eyes.

MICHAEL. Dean, don't.

DEAN. Michael, make me.

MICHAEL. I'm serious.

DEAN. No. You're trying to be serious, because the air of this whole debacle has a definite weight to it. But you want to smile.

MICHAEL. Maybe.

DEAN. It's okay to admit that you want to smile.

MICHAEL. Maybe I do.

DEAN. So do it.

MICHAEL. No. Not yet.

DEAN. Why?

MICHAEL. I don't know, just –

DEAN. Smile.

MICHAEL. I'm trying not to. I feel bad. We shouldn't be doing this.

DEAN. Doing what?

MICHAEL. Jane is – It just seems a bit off.

DEAN. We're allowed to talk, Michael.

MICHAEL. I'm not saying we shouldn't talk.

DEAN. We're allowed to smile.

MICHAEL. There is more to be settled first.

DEAN. Fine.

MICHAEL. Now you're being sullen.

DEAN. Yeah. I am.

MICHAEL. Why, because I'm not playing your little games?

DEAN. Yes. Because you're forcing yourself to be dreary. To be something you don't want to be.

MICHAEL. It seems wrong to giggle and fl – flirt with Jane right in the other room.

DEAN. Doing Lord knows what.

MICHAEL. I just feel weird about it. It's giving me the heebees.

DEAN. Fine. We'll talk about my thing.

MICHAEL. Yeah. Your thing.

DEAN. Not my thing-thing, but my –

MICHAEL. Deany. Stop it.

DEAN. My internship.

MICHAEL. Not your pants.

DEAN. My internship.

MICHAEL. You were a busy bee back before.

DEAN. Interning.

MICHAEL. Yes. The internship.

DEAN. It ended a month ago. Thanks for remembering.

MICHAEL. Did they hire you?

DEAN. No.

> (JANE *re-enters. She has re-done her hair, make-up and changed into a cocktail dress. Very "put together.")*

JANE. Eh hem. Here she is, boys.

MICHAEL. Lovely.

JANE. Thank you. There was something about that damn sweatshirt that just felt invasive. You know how it goes, Dean. You can enjoy something a lot and then all-the-sudden you just find it uncomfortable.

DEAN. Got it. Superiority intact, my dear. Michael has words to speak.

JANE. First time for everything. Are you actually going to include us this time?

MICHAEL. If you're going to try and demean my manner of dealing with this –

JANE. I'm not trying to demean anything –

MICHAEL. You might not be trying, but you're sure as shit succeeding. Knock it off for fifteen seconds and let's discuss this civilly.

DEAN. Civilly.

MICHAEL. Yes. Civilly.

JANE. Civilly.

DEAN. That is one of those words.

JANE. Civilly. Civilly. Civilly.

MICHAEL. Jesus.

DEAN. No, civilly.

JANE. Is the implication of that statement that I have begun to behave in a manner lacking civility?

MICHAEL. Stop it! Both of you.

—

Dean and I were walking by the river one afternoon and it started to rain so we got under this overhang thing and hung out for awhile.

JANE. A vestibule?

MICHAEL. We sat there for like two hours?

DEAN. And forty-five minutes.

MICHAEL. It was within the first half an hour that he asked me to be with him.

JANE. Marry. He said marry.

MICHAEL. I couldn't speak. I got nervous. I threw up on the side-walk.

DEAN. Charmer.

MICHAEL. It made sense in some way. It confused me but I didn't know how to say no.

JANE. You wanted to say yes.

MICHAEL. I couldn't stop myself.

JANE. You said yes? I'm so confused.

MICHAEL. Looking back, I realize that being presented with options, with a different future, I might also not be satisfied as one of three forever.

DEAN. And we have said a million times that we'd always be honest if this wasn't working any more –

JANE. Don't start. Your approach to all of this is another monster all together.

MICHAEL. I couldn't get myself to say no. Or yes. I told Dean that I'd think about it. We went over what it would really mean for us to be together alone.

JANE. You've never been together alone. It would not work.

DEAN. It could have. It kind of did –

MICHAEL. It was a few weeks two years ago and we didn't commit to each other until we committed to her.

—

Jane, Dean. What about Jane?

DEAN. I know. It's so hard.

MICHAEL. No, Dean. It's not hard. It's everything.

JANE. Thank you.

MICHAEL. I love her, Dean.

DEAN. So do I. Of course I do

—

JANE. – but you decided it was worth it not to have me in your life any longer.

DEAN. I weighed my options. I wasn't wholly happy with all of us and, despite my love for you, I thought that, if I could survive the transition period, I could be a happier person with Michael.

MICHAEL. But I didn't really say yes to him.

DEAN. Opposite.

JANE. And you disappeared.

MICHAEL. I meandered around alone and then came home to talk to both of you. Neither of you were here and the next thing I knew I was walking out of the building with a duffle over my shoulder and a toothbrush in my blazer pocket. I don't even remember packing it or choosing to pack it. I was just gone.

JANE. You left a note.

MICHAEL. I don't remember what I wrote.

JANE. "I'm going to be gone for a while. I don't think I can do this anymore. I love you. I'm sorry this went sour.

– M."

MICHAEL. You memorized it.

JANE. Not exactly a novel.

DEAN. After you left you went to a hotel.

MICHAEL. Let me talk, don't try and fill in the blanks for me.

DEAN. They're my blanks too.

MICHAEL. I asked him to give me a week and to start looking for a new place.

DEAN. For just the two of us.

MICHAEL. Dean. Let me say this.

JANE. So you did say yes?

DEAN. For like a minute.

MICHAEL. No!

DEAN. Sort of.

JANE & MICHAEL. SHUT UP.

MICHAEL. During that week, I went to work like normal and barely worked but didn't know what to do afterward. I felt, and still feel, this enormous amount of guilt.

JANE. Guilt? Me too.

MICHAEL. It hurts not to explain why I left, Jane. It burns my throat. I'm so sorry.

JANE. There are missing pieces here. The part where you decide not to come back to either of us and why you are here now.

MICHAEL. I don't know.

DEAN. What?

JANE. You don't know?

MICHAEL. Yes. That is what I said. I don't know.

JANE. He doesn't know. He doesn't know. Of course he doesn't know.

DEAN. What, Michael? Why did you leave? Why did you come back?

MICHAEL. Um – Fine.

JANE. What? You know something now? Come on!

MICHAEL. Maybe I slept with someone.

JANE. When?

MICHAEL. That week. That week at the hotel. I slept with someone else.

JANE. My throat burns.

DEAN. You never told me that

MICHAEL. I called Dean after it happened and told him that I'd changed my mind, and wouldn't be coming back.

DEAN. Oh my god. I knew it. I could just feel it.

MICHAEL. I just wanted to sleep with her so I did.

JANE. We all know how that goes.

DEAN. You needed an out.

MICHAEL. I didn't need an out. I wanted an in and couldn't find one.

DEAN. So you –

MICHAEL. – felt like nothing was my choice, Dean! You put me in this position of unavoidable failure. If I'd moved out of this apartment, home, and in with you somewhere else then I would have been completely betraying Jane. If I'd told you no then you would have been heartbroken and all of us would have been separated. There was absolutely no winning for me in that situation. And, honestly, all that makes me want to do is say 'fuck you'! Fuck you. Seriously. How dare you put me in that position? How dare you? Selfish.

DEAN. So you go out and fuck some random –

MICHAEL. Yes. Yes that is exactly what I did. It's my body and I can do whatever I want with it. I'm not going to apologize for that. You're so weird about sex. It was just sex.

DEAN. This stings. I keep shaking.

JANE. You let what we say and feel affect everything you do.

MICHAEL. We have each other in these glass cases. We don't own each other.

DEAN. It means that I have empathy.

MICHAEL. It bothers you to know that I could sleep with someone else while you're not there.

DEAN. I just want to be a part of it. I'm not like you. It's not just sex to me.

MICHAEL. Exactly. It bothers you.

JANE. I think we've gotten off track. Again.

MICHAEL. Surely.

DEAN. Laverne.

MICHAEL. Good one.

JANE. Let's get back to before, Michael. Why'd you come back?

MICHAEL. I'm still in love with you.

JANE. Me?

MICHAEL. I'm in love with you, Dean, and I love you Jane.

JANE. That shit is getting old real fast. I love you but I'm not in love with you.

MICHAEL. Jane.

JANE. Michael, please stop addressing me right now.

DEAN. Michael.

MICHAEL. No. We haven't talked but I still feel you with me. Like we're on pause. I knew we'd have this moment. No matter how many good days I have by myself there are always more bad days.

DEAN. Aching feelings in the creases of my elbows because I miss you so badly.

MICHAEL. When I imagine the kind of person I want to be with, I end up with all these little pieces that make someone just like you. They look like you, they have your beliefs, they like the things you like.

Dean, when you asked me to marry you it felt weird but I couldn't say no.

I never stopped caring about you, Jane. I'll never stop.
But something doesn't click the way it used to.

JANE. I don't think I can do this conversation anymore.
I think I'm going to be sick.

MICHAEL. Jane, I'm sorry. We're just trying to be honest.

DEAN. And apparently it just comes spilling out. It spews.

JANE. This sucks – I, um, but wait – oh god. I can't breathe!
I can't breathe – I –

> *(She is hyper-ventilating. Without missing a beat,*
> **DEAN** *runs into the kitchen and* **MICHAEL** *goes to*
> **JANE** *and hugs her in front of him tightly.* **DEAN**
> *comes back in with a wet towel and grabs* **JANE***'s*
> *hands.)*

JANE. Please don't touch me!

> **(DEAN** *lets go of* **JANE,** **MICHAEL** *is still holding*
> *her.)*

DEAN. Janey-baby.

> **(JANE** *lets out a scream that could shatter steel.)*

> *(Her soul from her throat. She has broken.)*

MICHAEL. Dean.

JANE. Let go of me!!

MICHAEL. Okay.

> *(He lets go.)*

Okay.

DEAN. You're the most amazing woman. You know this. You
are the most amazing woman I could possibly imagine.

JANE. This all feels like such bullshit.

MICHAEL. It's not bullshit.

DEAN. I love you, Jane.

MICHAEL. What else is there to say that hasn't been said?

JANE. The truth.

MICHAEL. We're telling the truth, Jane. That's why this is
so awkward.

JANE. But what about my truth? Don't I get a say?

DEAN. Of course you get a say.

JANE. Okay. Well my, um, my – wait – my truth is that I want to go back in time and stop this from happening at all. Stop myself from being such a slut and agreeing to sleep with two gay guys and then falling for them and letting myself believe that I had transcended some –

DEAN. Don't call yourself a slut –

JANE. Don't interrupt me! I thought we'd found something. It's not fair. You got me into this mess. You started it. You did. Not me.

You're my family. Michael, Dean. You became my world. The rest of the world, our old friends and boyfriends and lives, it all just washed away and we became something new. New and fucking glorious if I do say so myself. Absolutely glorious.

But now I learn that it just poof-changed. It changed for you and it changed for you, but it didn't change for me. I didn't get a say. I didn't get an opportunity to choose something else for myself. I'm being told that my relationship is over and I don't have any say. I don't get to argue my side of the good times or my side of what could be if we keep trying because you've both already decided that you don't want me anymore.

DEAN. We love you but maybe you're right.

MICHAEL. Relationships end and it sucks.

JANE. Well the actuality of it, the technicality of it, the fact of it, the logistics of it is awful. It's not fair and it's especially unfair that I am supposed to just accept. Just open my eyes and accept what my life has become.

DEAN. You need to know that I do love you, Jane.

JANE. Stop saying that! You say it over and over and it doesn't mean anything anymore. Stop it. I never want to hear that stupid fucking word. How did this become all about me being left alone? Can we stop, now? Please? I have nothing else to say. I have to stop. This has to stop.

DEAN. – Are we done?

JANE. No.

MICHAEL. What do we have left?

JANE. Well, you two have to make nice and get together, right?

DEAN. That would seem appropriate.

MICHAEL. Jane, I don't want to have this conversation in front of you. I feel like it's hurting you.

DEAN. I don't want to hurt you.

JANE. You know what? I have a feeling that watching the two of you have this conversation would be much better than trying to make it up in my head.

MICHAEL. Okay.

DEAN. Okay.

MICHAEL. Are you sure?

JANE. Go.

MICHAEL. Okay. Dean.
I've been sitting in an apartment thinking about the two of you for three months and it has been really difficult for me.

DEAN. Me too.

MICHAEL. I know.

DEAN. I've been with Jane. We've been doing okay. We've been making do. It wasn't some sort of fairy-tale pairing, but we've been doing good.

MICHAEL. Yes.

DEAN. She and I had sex without you.

MICHAEL. I imagined. Tried to pretend that it wasn't happening.

JANE. It was weird the first time.

DEAN. A little.

JANE. Maybe even forced.

DEAN. Forced sounds wrong, I think.

JANE. Mutually forced.

DEAN. Not forced. Challenging.

JANE. Sure.

DEAN. It got better.

MICHAEL. Okay.

DEAN. It was good. Sometimes seemingly perfect.

JANE. Good sex. Boom.

DEAN. I just need you to know that. We always said we'd tell each other if just two of us slept together.

MICHAEL. You don't owe me anything.

DEAN. You slept with that chick. You told us.

MICHAEL. About that. I –

DEAN. Is that it? She was the only one?

MICHAEL. Yeah. Sure.

DEAN. Okay. And now we're here. What do you want, Michael?

MICHAEL. What do you mean?

DEAN. From me.

MICHAEL. I want to be with you.

JANE. I need a refill.

DEAN. I love that –

JANE. On second thought, maybe I should leave. This is awful.

DEAN. Don't.

MICHAEL. Let her go. She doesn't need to torture herself.

DEAN. Just wait.

JANE. Dean, really.

DEAN. Please stay for a moment. I want you to really know the ending.

MICHAEL. Okay. What else is there to say?

JANE. "I love you, Dean."

"I love you, Michael."

DEAN. I don't want that.

MICHAEL. I'm sorry?

DEAN. I don't want to be with you.

Oh God. I've been doing too much thinking and
explaining and understanding and hurting for too long.
I'm confused. I don't want to be with you anymore.
I just decided. I don't want to be with you anymore.
I did until probably thirty minutes ago but hearing you
say that you wanted to be with me it just – it hit me.
I think about you constantly but now that you're here
and now that I could touch you again. I don't want to.
I think we need a little independence.

MICHAEL. No. No, Dean. I think you misunderstood me.
I think you don't understand what I want for us. I want
the ring.

DEAN. No I get it. I really get it. I get it so much.

MICHAEL. Deany, wait –

DEAN. I have to go. I don't know what to do with my body
anymore. I'm not – I don't want to sit around anymore
describing all of this.

JANE. This sucks.

DEAN. I'm just being honest.

JANE. Familiar.

DEAN. I never asked you to be with me again, Michael. You
left and I feel messy.

MICHAEL. Can we pause.

JANE. Pause.

MICHAEL. What about a kiss? We could hate it, I realize
that. I do.

DEAN. No.

MICHAEL. Please.

DEAN. No. I'm going to keep moving. Maybe we just didn't
give ourselves enough time to get over this. Goodnight,
Michael. I'll talk to you soon? Jane, "hey" to the folks.
Goodbye. I'm sorry. Goodbye.

(DEAN *leaves.*)

MICHAEL. He left.

JANE. Familiar.

MICHAEL. He left.

JANE. Get used to it.

MICHAEL. Jane.

JANE. I'm going to take a shower.

MICHAEL. What are we supposed to do?

JANE. Get over it.

MICHAEL. Get over it.

JANE. Get over it or – or get over it. Options.

MICHAEL. Jane. What's happening right now?

JANE. We just got dumped, boy.

MICHAEL. It's really over this time.

JANE. Yeah.

MICHAEL. I – I, um.

Wait, so, but, um –

JANE. Sorry, Michael.

Love you.

> *(JANE exits. MICHAEL is left alone. He grabs a blanket and pulls it over his body. He holds it close to his face.)*

—

MICHAEL. The first time I – My lungs are in my throat.

The first time I met Dean we were on an airplane and he pretended to fall onto me to get my attention. I've always known that he'd be there when I was ready for him, that's why I took my time.

I really fucked this up didn't I?

—

> *(MICHAEL squirms.)*

Jane? Janey? Can I come in?

> *(He walks out of the room towards JANE. The stage is empty for a short moment and the lights fade to black.)*

End of Play